No AR

W9-DJG-601

Careers For
The Curious

Interviews by Russell Shorto

Photographs by Edward Keating and Carrie Boretz

CHOICES
The Millbrook Press
Brookfield, Connecticut

Produced in association with Agincourt Press.

Choices Editor: Megan Liberman

Photographs by Edward Keating, except: Daniel N. Pagano (Carrie
Boretz), Adelaida Reyes Schramm (Carrie Boretz), Micheline Blum
(Carrie Boretz), Paula G. Rubel (Carrie Boretz), Robert Yates (Steve
Kagan), Laura Flax (Gary Eisenberg).

Library of Congress Cataloging-in-Publication Data

Shorto, Russell.
Careers for the curious/interviews by Russell Shorto,
photographs by Edward Keating and Carrie Boretz.

p.   cm. — (Choices)
Includes bibliographic references and index.

Summary: People who like to use their minds, including an antique
collector, opinion researcher, and detective, describe what they do in
their jobs, how they got there, and what others would need to get a
similar job.

ISBN 1-56294-064-3

1. Vocational guidance — United States — Juvenile literature.
2. Occupations — United States — Juvenile literature.
3. Professions — United States — Juvenile literature.
4. Professional employees — United States — Interviews.
[1. Occupations.   2. Vocational guidance.]
I. Keating, Edward, ill.   II. Boretz, Carrie, ill.
III. Title.   IV. Series: Choices (Brookfield, Conn.)
HF5381.2.S543   1992   91-47145
331.7'02 — dc20

Contents

Introduction 5

URBAN ARCHAEOLOGIST: Daniel N. Pagano 6

ETHNOMUSICOLOGIST: Adelaida Reyes Schramm 10

SPECIAL WARFARE OFFICER: Lt. Cmdr. Joseph Kernan 14

ASTROPHYSICIST: Jeff Goldstein 18

OPINION RESEARCHER: Micheline Blum 22

DETECTIVE: Chief Aaron H. Rosenthal 26

ANTHROPOLOGIST: Paula G. Rubel 30

ETHNOBOTANIST: Mark Plotkin 34

MANAGEMENT CONSULTANT: Jill Storey 38

MATHEMATICIAN: John Garnett 42

ANTIQUES DEALER: Roberta Dean 46

MANAGING EDITOR: Robert Yates 50

INVENTOR: Laura Flax 54

PHILOSOPHER: Paul Richard Warren 58

Related Careers 61

Further Information About Careers For The Curious 62

Glossary Index 64

Introduction

In this book, fourteen people who work in research-related jobs talk about their careers — what their work involves, how they got started, and what they like (and dislike) about it. They tell you things you should know before beginning an investigative career and show you how being curious can lead to many different types of jobs.

Many of the people featured in this book work in traditional academic careers, such as anthropologist, mathematician, and philosopher. Others — including the opinion researcher, the management consultant, and the inventor — use their investigative skills in private enterprise. Still others — such as the detective, the urban archaeologist, and the special warfare officer — work as public servants. And some satisfy their natural curiosity in much more unconventional careers, such as ethnobotanist and ethnomusicologist.

The fourteen careers described here are just the beginning, so don't limit your sights. At the end of this book, you'll find short descriptions of a dozen more careers you may want to explore, as well as suggestions on how to get more information. There are many business opportunities for people with curious minds. If you're so inclined, you'll find a wide range of career choices open to you.

Joan E. Storey, M.B.A., M.S.W.
Series Career Consultant

"I always liked to dig."

DANIEL N. PAGANO

URBAN ARCHAEOLOGIST

New York, New York

WHAT I DO:

As the city's archaeologist, I manage New York's vast archaeological heritage. New York City's prehistory covers about 12,000 years of Native American settlement. Then there are about 350 years of historical archaeology, which start with the Dutch contact in the early 1600s.

Broadly speaking, archaeology is the scientific study of the past. The prefix *archae-* means *ancient.* Archaeologists look at the past in order to learn more about humankind. The ultimate purpose of archaeology, I believe, is to help us to live better in the future.

Like all archaeologists, I do a lot of research, which can include consulting maps and historical documents as well as going out into the field to locate and investigate

Daniel oversees an excavation before construction begins.

sites of historic importance. Sometimes we find out about sites that are in danger. A developer, for instance, may be preparing to put up a new office building on a historic- ally significant site.

In these cases, my job is to preserve the city's heritage by retrieving as many arti- facts as possible before the site is destroyed. I require the developer to hire an archaeological team to inves- tigate the site. I oversee their work as they probe beneath the pavement, searching for artifacts. Then we study our findings, looking for clues to the site's significance and what else we might find there. Finally we decide whether or not to perform a full-scale excavation.

In a city like New York, there are a wide variety of sites to be found. On Staten Island, for example, there's a Native American burial ground, which has been set aside as a nature preserve and park. Because New York has long been a port city, we've also discovered a number of sunken ships off shore. These are important because they tell us a great deal about the culture and trade of New York at different points in history.

HOW I GOT STARTED:
As a kid, I loved spending time outdoors, uncovering things. I would pedal around the neighborhood on my bicycle and collect garbage to see what other people had discarded. I always liked to dig. I loved the smell of the earth and the thrill of discovery.

One summer, while I was in college, I went on an archaeological dig and realized that I could do this for a living. I decided to major in anthropology, and then I went on to get a master's degree in anthropological archaeology. Now I'm working on my Ph.D.

HOW I FEEL ABOUT IT:
I think this is absolutely the most fun thing I could do. Archaeology is like detective work. You're always searching for answers to questions about the past. And as soon as you answer one question, another one pops up.

I also enjoy the teamwork. In addition to archaeologists

Daniel talks to a contract archaeologist at a site.

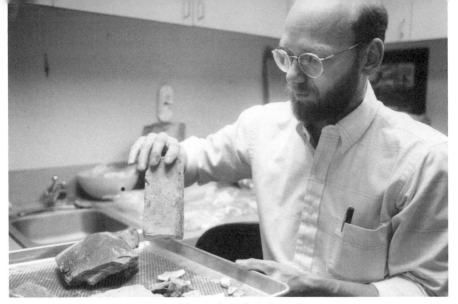

Daniel looks over some artifacts in his laboratory.

on a dig, you might also find a botanist, a chemist, a computer scientist, and an artist to draw the artifacts. It's great fun working with such diverse people.

WHAT YOU SHOULD KNOW: I would recommend getting a broad liberal arts education in college. Archaeology is an interdisciplinary field, which means that you have to know about a number of different subjects. So take a wide variety of courses. Then you'll be ready to do your graduate work in archaeology. You should also like being a problem solver and an investigator.

Archaeologists are employed in many areas, especially by governmental agencies such as the National Park Service and state parks systems. You can also do university work, of course. Then there's contract archaeology, which involves doing research for real estate developers who need to conduct archaeological surveys of the sites of proposed building projects. There's also a lot of museum work available.

You can make a decent living at this work, but personal growth and development are the real reasons to do it, because money can't buy that kind of satisfaction. In terms of a salary range, you can expect to earn $8 to $10 an hour working on a dig without a master's degree. As you get more training, however, you can work your way up to about $30,000 a year. As a college professor, you start at about $35,000 a year. The longer you work in the field, the more you'll make.

"I've done fieldwork with refugees in camps around the world."

ADELAIDA REYES SCHRAMM
ETHNO-MUSICOLOGIST
Leonia, New Jersey

WHAT I DO:

I study music and musical behavior wherever it occurs. My field is called ethno-musicology, which is the study of music in its social and cultural context. I started in New York City, studying black and Hispanic populations in East Harlem. Now I'm working with Vietnamese refugees. I've done fieldwork with refugees in camps around the world as well as here in the United States.

I started by interviewing Vietnamese refugees in New York. I talked with them about their experiences escaping from Vietnam and the effect those experiences have had on them. Next, I traveled to Vietnamese refugee camps in Hong Kong and the Philippines, where I lived with the refugees in

Adelaida records a live band playing at an outdoor concert.

the camps. I observed the way they adapted to camp life and the effect it had on their music. Finally I followed the refugees to their new homes. I went to Orange County, California, where many of the refugees have settled, and there I did my most recent fieldwork.

To many Vietnamese, music isn't just entertainment; it's also a political expression. These Vietnamese divide everything, including music, into Communist and non-Communist affiliations. In fact, there are great efforts now to preserve the music of Vietnam from before 1975, when Vietnam became a single, Communist country.

The attachment these people feel to pre-1975 Vietnam manifests itself in unusual ways, such as a devotion to the tango. The tango is not a traditional Vietnamese dance; rather, it was brought to Vietnam

Adelaida attends a music festival in New York.

through contact with the French and Americans during the 1950s and 1960s. Because it was part of Vietnam's pre-Communist life, however, people feel that the tango should be preserved. Now, when they celebrate traditional Asian feasts, the Vietnamese refugees always dance the tango.

HOW I GOT STARTED:

I was born in the Philippines, and I went to a music conservatory in Manila, where I learned the music of the great Western composers — Bach, Beethoven, Brahms, and so on. After school, I got a job as a music critic for a Philippine newspaper. Then I got a fellowship from the Rockefeller Foundation in New York to study music criticism. The foundation also asked me to evaluate ethnomusicology programs that had applied to them for grants. This was my first exposure to ethnomusicology, and it attracted me very much, because it involved music in a variety of contexts, not just concert halls. I decided that this was the field I wanted to pursue, so I found a program that I liked at Columbia University and enrolled in graduate studies there.

HOW I FEEL ABOUT IT:

I adore my work. It brings me into contact with a wide variety of people. It also makes me see music in far more dimensions than I might have had I stayed with the regular conservatory training.

There are some difficulties, however. Because ethnomusicology is a fairly new field, many institutions don't really understand it yet. Western musicologists study "the great works," whereas ethnomusicologists study all music — from folk music to rock — without attempting to judge which works or styles are superior. Because Western musicology dominates most music departments many people still believe that ethnomusicology is an inferior discipline.

WHAT YOU SHOULD KNOW: First it's important to know the music of your own culture as thoroughly as possible. If you have grown up with Western music, learn it well. But you should also be open to other kinds of music, even those you don't think you like. You need to stretch your ears and your mind. In college, it would be a good idea to combine a major in music with courses in anthropology, sociology, and linguistics.

The money is very hard to characterize, because there is such a wide range of things that ethnomusicologists do. Some work in museums, others for public interest groups. But most teach at colleges and universities and are paid as professors. Ethnomusicologists who have been in the field for a long time earn an average of $60,000 to $65,000 a year.

Adelaida studies all different kinds of music.

"Often you're placed in life-or-death situations, so you have to be cool under pressure."

SPECIAL WARFARE OFFICER

Washington, D.C.

WHAT I DO:

I'm a U.S. Navy SEAL, which stands for Sea, Air, and Land. The job of the SEALs is to support U.S. military operations, whether they're launched by the army, the navy, or both. We're the naval counterpart to the army's Green Berets, but we go in behind enemy lines before anyone else. Our job might be to destroy a designated warfare target or to clear an area of beach in advance of an assault.

We also gather intelligence behind the lines so assault commanders can know what to expect before they begin a major action. We inform them about enemy forces at the chosen point of attack, as well as about the numbers and locations of other enemy personnel, anti-aircraft guns, weapons, and radar sites.

Joseph waits outside his office at a Washington naval base.

Naval special warfare is a distinct career path in the military, and it's the one I've chosen. You have to be accepted to, and then complete, a six-month training course, which is very physically demanding — only 20 to 50 percent of those who begin complete it. After the course, you go to jump school, which is army airborne training, where you learn to parachute from a plane.

You need all sorts of skills to do this work, many of which are survival skills. For example, you have to be a good swimmer, because it might take you three hours to reach your landing point. And when you go in behind enemy lines, you have to carry enough equipment to live for up to ten days on your own. Also, if you're behind the lines, you often can't go to sleep. So the training for this work includes sleep deprivation. We have what's called "Hell Week" — a whole week during which we get only two to four hours of sleep.

We also learn to take photographs at night, how to sketch a target, and how to identify foreign weapons, tanks, and aircraft. Today many Navy SEALs also learn foreign languages.

HOW I GOT STARTED:

I grew up in Florida, where I lived close to the ocean, and I was always drawn to the water. When I heard about the SEALs, I knew this was what I wanted to do. I went to the Naval Academy out of high school. My first assignment was as a surface warfare officer, working as an engineer on a guided-missile cruiser. Then I applied to the SEALs. It took me three tries to get accepted, because surface warfare needed engineers and couldn't afford to let me go.

Once I got into the SEALs, I began working overseas in a cross-training program with the British, Koreans, Thais, and others. Then I became a platoon commander.

HOW I FEEL ABOUT IT:

I wouldn't trade my job for anything. I especially love the active part of the work. As I gain seniority, though, I don't get as many operational assignments. My work

Joseph is always practicing his diving skills.

Joseph relaxes with two of his fellow Navy SEALS.

is more administrative now. But even so, I still enjoy it. There are only five hundred of us in the SEALs, and everybody knows everybody. It's really like a family.

WHAT YOU SHOULD KNOW: This work is both physically and mentally demanding. There's a lot of stress in this job. Often you're placed in life-or-death situations, so you have to be cool under pressure. You also have to be in good physical condition to be in the SEALs. Even our admirals maintain their jump qualifications. And you need to be mature and responsible, because you do a lot of work on your own, and you may have to lead others.

It helps to have a strong interest in travel, because much of your work will be overseas. And, of course, you have to be water-oriented. We spend a lot of time in the water.

In terms of salary, we do better than most military careers because, in addition to regular navy pay, we're also eligible for diving pay, jump pay, and demolition pay, all of which fall under the category of hazardous duty pay. The base salary is about $20,000 a year. But with hazardous duty pay added on, you might make 15 to 20 percent more than that. Still, it's not a job people stay in for the money. They do it because they love the work.

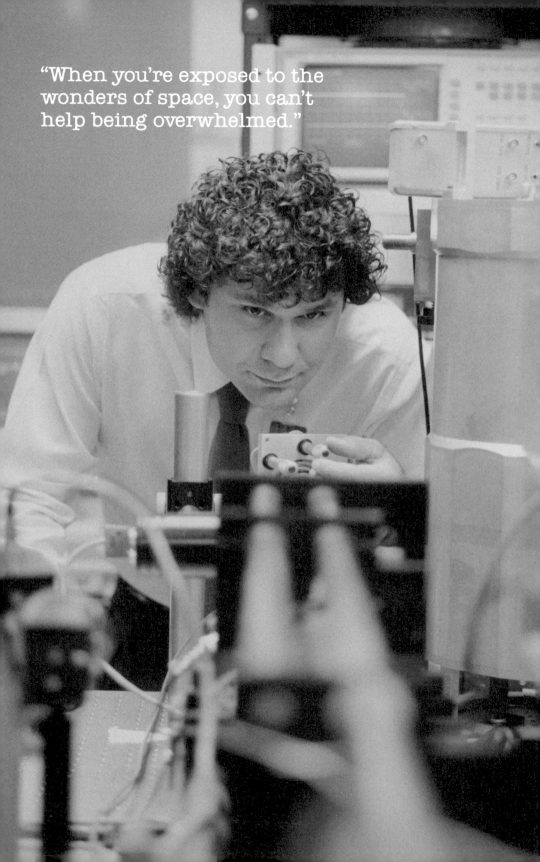

"When you're exposed to the wonders of space, you can't help being overwhelmed."

JEFF GOLDSTEIN

ASTROPHYSICIST

Washington, D.C.

WHAT I DO:
I work for the Smithsonian Institution's National Air and Space Museum. The museum has four research wings, and I am in the wing called the Laboratory for Astrophysics. I use astrophysical techniques to study wind dynamics on other planets. Essentially, I'm an interplanetary weatherman.

I measure the speed of winds on other planets, using an instrument called an infrared superheterodyne spectrometer. By studying the behavior of these winds, we learn more about the properties of weather in general, including weather on the earth. Studying the differences and similarities among planets is called comparative planetology, and that's what I do. The earth is just one planet, and each planet is different. Essentially, each planet has its own personality.

We use some of the world's largest telescopes, including the National Aeronautics and Space Administration (NASA) Infrared Telescope Facility on top of Mauna Kea, in Hawaii. Mauna Kea reaches an elevation of 14,000 feet, so you suffer from oxygen deprivation up there, which can be hard on the body. We go out for two weeks at a time to conduct experiments, and for the first few days we're always sick to our stomachs. But it's worth the trouble. Working on the frontier of space exploration is an unforgettable and moving experience.

HOW I GOT STARTED:
When I was about 7, I looked up and saw a glowing object sail across the daytime sky. It turned out to be a meteor, and it fascinated me. Then,

Jeff adjusts an instrument that measures wind speed.

19

on July 20, 1969, when I was 11, my family moved to New York. I can remember sitting on moving boxes that day and staring at the television set in awe. It was the day that Neil Armstrong set foot on the moon. I knew then that space science was the field I wanted to pursue. I never really considered anything else. And the lesson here, I think, is that you're never too young to understand what it is you want to do.

HOW I FEEL ABOUT IT:

In addition to my work, I also give lectures to students and teachers. I do one called "How Big Is Big," which is an imaginary journey from the earth out to the farthest reaches of the universe. I've given it dozens of times, and every time I give it I'm still incredibly awed by the majesty of the subject. No matter how much education has been pumped into your head, when you're exposed to the wonders of space, you can't help being overwhelmed.

This work gives you a unique vantage point from which to consider the earth. When you look at the earth as a planet, you realize that it doesn't have infinite horizons, but is instead a single, fragile environment. Seeing the earth from space, national

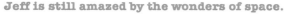
Jeff is still amazed by the wonders of space.

By studying other planets, Jeff learns about the earth.

borders seem to disappear, and all of the things that people fight over seem so insignificant. I'm not really a religious person, but to study this planet on the grandest of scales is truly a religious experience.

WHAT YOU SHOULD KNOW: Study the physical sciences and mathematics. It's never too early to start. Don't wait until the end of high school or college. The more time you spend developing basic math and science skills, the better off you'll be.

Also, visit a local planetarium or university and talk to the people who work there. Universities and planetariums have done a great deal to make themselves accessible

to young people who are interested in space. You can also try talking to government researchers. Go to NASA installations, for instance, and talk to the scientists there. You can find out where these NASA centers are at your local library. And even if there aren't any NASA centers near you, you can write to one or call. Don't be bashful. It's important to talk to people in the field so that you get an accurate image of what we do.

The money isn't great in this work. As a college professor, you might start at about $25,000 a year. Right now, I'm making $34,000 a year. But you don't do this for the money. You do it for the personal rewards.

"I always want to know more than I can possibly find out."

MICHELINE BLUM

OPINION RESEARCHER

New York, New York

WHAT I DO:
I conduct public opinion surveys. My work involves asking people questions on all sorts of subjects, analyzing the results, and presenting the findings to my clients, who are mostly television networks and newspapers. My partner and I have our own company, and we hire other people to work for us when we need them.

There are several stages to this work, and coming up with the questions is one of them. It's very important to ask unbiased questions. You can't lead people into an answer, or you'll get unreliable results

For example, not many people will say that they find math interesting if you ask a question like, "Don't you think math is boring?" A better question would be, "Do

you think math is: very interesting, somewhat interesting, not interesting?" That way, you'll get a better idea of how people really feel.

Sampling, or choosing the people you will question, is another important part of polling. The idea is to pick a sample of people that is truly representative of the whole group you want to survey. Otherwise, again, the results won't be accurate.

Today, polls are done for many different reasons. A television network might do an audience research poll to find out what kinds of programs people like and want to see more of. Or a politician may want to know how his constituents feel about a particular issue. But some polls are done just out of curiosity, to find out what other people think. Certainly people who go into this work are curious about what other people think.

Micheline writes the questions for a poll she's conducting.

Micheline reads over a returned questionnaire.

HOW I GOT STARTED:

After I graduated from college, I worked on a number of political campaigns before going back to graduate school to study psychological measurement and statistics. Then, one day, I got a call from someone I had worked with in politics. She was working for a television news department at the time, and her network was looking for someone with experience in both politics and statistics. I was offered a job in polling and election coverage, and I worked there for eleven years. It was a much bigger operation than my business is now. During elections, I managed as many as five thousand people.

HOW I FEEL ABOUT IT:

When I'm working on a project, I really do love it. I like writing the questions and then doing the detective work to find out who thinks what. I always want to know more than I can possibly find out. But there's a limit, after all, to how many questions you can ask a person. I also like the surprises, the unexpected results you find in every poll.

Being in business for yourself can be difficult, however. There are times when work is hard to find, when all you do is write proposals. Trying to get clients is the part I'm not crazy about. Still, working for yourself can be more interesting than working for a big company because the work is more varied. If you work for, say, a network news organization, you tend to do only one kind of polling. Working for yourself, though, you can do many different kinds.

WHAT YOU SHOULD KNOW: Often high school and college kids can find part-time work doing telephone polling, especially as an election year approaches. It can be a good way for young people to explore the field.

Traditionally, the ticket into the polling business is a political science degree. But you can also enter the field from the other social sciences, such as sociology and psychology, which deal with related issues. Most colleges also offer courses in survey research.

Salaries in this field vary a lot. Once you get into a managerial position in polling, you can make between $50,000 and $70,000 a year, but starting out you'll only make around $30,000 a year. If you have your own business, there really is no standard salary. In the beginning, you may even lose money. But for the heavy hitters, the sky's the limit.

Micheline talks to one of her clients about a poll.

"I've made some very dramatic arrests in my career."

CHIEF AARON H. ROSENTHAL

DETECTIVE

New York, New York

WHAT I DO:

I'm the commanding officer of the support services bureau for the police department of the City of New York. I deal with all the drugs, guns, and cars that are used in crimes. I'm also in charge of central records, which is the department responsible for fingerprinting. Until recently, however, I was the commanding officer of Detective Borough Manhattan, and I still see myself as a detective.

As head of detectives, I supervised every squad in Manhattan. Detectives are responsible for handling crimes such as assaults, robberies, burglaries, and murders. Every such crime in Manhattan, once it was reported, became my responsibility. I had to ensure that the investigations were

Aaron is in charge of the city's central records office.

conducted properly, that no details were overlooked, and that the detectives operated within constitutional limits.

There are many steps involved in investigating a crime. Once a crime is reported, uniformed officers in the area respond to the call, and then they bring in the detective squad for that precinct. Once the detectives are called in, they begin examining the scene and looking for clues and witnesses.

Each type of crime is different. If it's a murder case, the body is examined before it's brought to the morgue. For a robbery case, detectives try to track down the stolen items at pawnshops.

It's important to study the scene of a crime so that you get some sense of what was happening as the crime took place. I once had a case, for example, in which a man was murdered in his own

Aaron deals with all the guns used in crimes.

apartment. It was clear to me that whoever killed this guy had stayed around for a while. They had used the refrigerator and the television, so I thought maybe they had used the phone, too. It turned out that they had, and we caught them by tracing their call.

HOW I GOT STARTED:
I was an officer in the air force, and when I got out, good jobs were hard to come by. A friend of mine was applying to the police department, and he convinced me to take the test with him. I wasn't really thrilled with the idea at first, but I figured I had nothing to lose. As it turned out, my friend failed and I passed. I've been with the department for forty years now.

I started out as a foot cop in Harlem, but I moved up quickly. I made a lot of arrests, some in very important cases, and I already had a college degree, so I was promoted to detective in the Bronx bureau. Later I was appointed to captain of detectives in the Bronx before I became head of detectives in Manhattan.

HOW I FEEL ABOUT IT:
Sometimes I think that I was made for this work. Growing up as a street kid in the Bronx, I was alert and knew

the city. So when I first became a cop, I used to say that I was still hanging out on street corners, only now I was getting paid for it.

Being a detective can be incredibly exciting work. Sometimes you get a case with no leads and you have to puzzle through it — it's quite a challenge. I've made some very dramatic arrests in my career. And as a detective, I've worked on some of the most highly publicized cases in the city. I'm even writing a book about my experiences.

WHAT YOU SHOULD KNOW: Policing is a great career, but don't think it's anything like "Hill Street Blues." If you're interested, talk to police officers and get all the litera-ture you can. That's the only way to find out what the work is really like. Movies and television don't show the downside — working all night, dealing with dead bodies, carrying people into ambulances, and so on. It isn't all fun and games.

Financially, there are a lot of benefits to being a cop. For one, the police cadet corps in New York will help pay for your college education, and then when you graduate, you've got a job on the force. The starting salary for a New York City police officer is $29,000 a year, and after five years on the force, you earn about $44,000 a year. You also get paid vacations, a full benefits package, a clothing allowance, holiday bonuses, and overtime pay.

Aaron talks to one of his colleagues on the force.

"Anthropologists are the kind of people who have always been interested in faraway places."

PAULA G. RUBEL

ANTHROPOLOGIST

New York, New York

WHAT I DO:

Anthropologists study the origins and behavior of humans. There are four traditional fields of anthropology: cultural anthropology, which is the study of human culture; physical anthropology, which concerns human biology; linguistic anthropology, which deals with human language; and archaeology, which helps us learn about ancient cultures through the study of artifacts.

I'm a cultural anthropologist. The most important things that cultural anthropologists study are how different cultures operate and how sensitivity to these differences makes it easier for people to understand their own culture. I'm also a professor of anthropology at a university, teaching both undergraduate and graduate courses.

Fieldwork is basic to what cultural anthropologists do. It involves traveling to and living within the culture you want to study. This includes doing what's called participant observation – which is observing the people of a society while at the same time participating in their cultural life. You live with the people, eat with them, go to their weddings and funerals, and so on. In this way, fieldwork gives you a first-hand knowledge and understanding of other people that you couldn't get from a book.

My work involves more than just looking at a culture today, however, because to understand the way a culture operates now, you have to look at its history. This can mean a lot of research in archives and libraries that preserve the journals of travelers.

Paula studies one of the artifacts she collected on an island near New Guinea.

Right now, I'm doing research on the history of contacts between the people of New Ireland, an island in the southwest Pacific Ocean near New Guinea, and the Europeans who visited the island in the 17th century, as well as those who colonized it two hundred years later. There is archaeological evidence that New Ireland was inhabited 30,000 years ago. But where did those inhabitants come from? And what language did they speak? These are the kinds of questions that cultural anthropologists try to answer.

HOW I GOT STARTED:
I majored in psychology in college, where I took only two courses in anthropology.

After I graduated, I thought about going on to graduate work in social psychology, but there were no Ph.D. programs in that field, so I decided to switch to anthropology instead and got my doctorate in that.

Anthropologists are usually the kind of people who have always been interested in faraway places and the people who live there. Also, anthropologists are typically not very strongly anchored to their own cultures, which makes them ideally suited to the work of exploring other cultures. I suppose I've always been like this myself.

HOW I FEEL ABOUT IT:
I wouldn't do anything else. Although it's very hard work,

Paula teaches a college seminar in anthropology.

Paula's work involves a lot of library research.

it provides constant intellectual stimulation. I know that I'll never be able to read enough or learn enough in my lifetime, but I try anyway. New avenues of interest are always opening up.

The part of the job I enjoy least is having to mark students' papers. I like teaching, but marking papers and the other bureaucratic work you have to do as a college professor often gets tiresome.

WHAT YOU SHOULD KNOW:
If you're interested in other cultures, look into anthropology. Some high schools even offer courses in the subject. Then when you're in college, take courses in anthropology and related fields as well, such as political science. After that, apply to a graduate program. You need a lot of schooling to do this work. It's almost impossible to work in anthropology without a Ph.D.

Even with all that schooling, however, you don't make much money in anthropology. Professors such as myself make what all academics make, starting at $30,000 a year or so for an assistant professor. There are lots of people who major in anthropology, however, who don't continue in the field, but who use what they learn here in legal, business, and medical careers.

"You have to be willing to be uncomfortable — to sleep in a hammock, drink muddy water, and eat disgusting foods."

MARK PLOTKIN
ETHNOBOTANIST
Washington, D.C.

WHAT I DO:
I work with tribal peoples in the Amazon, gathering information about the tropical plants they use. I study these plants because they're incredible storehouses of scientifically useful chemicals that are often impossible to find anywhere else.

Ethnobotanists learn about plants by watching native peoples use them. Often the ways in which they use these plants suggest ways we can use them in our own society. The rosy periwinkle, for example, has long been used by local people in Madagascar to treat disease. Now a chemical derived from that plant has become a leading anti-cancer drug.

Since 1978, I've been working in the northeast Amazon, the area where

Suriname, Brazil, Venezuela, and Guyana all join together. It's one of the most remote regions in the world. I go into the jungle and live with the native Indians who teach me about the local plants they use. Then I bring back samples of the plants so that they can be studied more closely in the lab.

Some scientists work exclusively in laboratories synthesizing new drugs, but ethnobotanists still believe that Mother Nature is a much better chemist. In fact, we've only just begun to explore all her creations, which is one reason why it's so important that we preserve the environment. Allowing farmers to burn down rain forests, for example, could cost us a cure for AIDS or cancer, a new biodegradable pesticide, new foods to feed the hungry, or wonderful new spices to vary our diet. It could all go up in smoke.

Mark looks at a sculpture he obtained during a field trip.

35

Mark talks to a native about the plants he uses.

HOW I GOT STARTED:

I dropped out of college because I wasn't sure what I wanted to study. I went to work for a museum instead. I met some people who were studying plants. Soon I became fascinated with their work. The museum sent me to the Amazon to chase lizards, but I was more interested in the tropical plants there. I went back to school, finished college, and then got a master's degree in forestry and a Ph.D. in conservation biology.

HOW I FEEL ABOUT IT:

This isn't a "punch the clock" job — it's a commitment.

I eat, sleep, breathe, and live this stuff. I deal with all kinds of people — from Amazonian witch doctors to presidents of major corporations to movie stars who have committed themselves to helping us get the public interested in the environment.

I guess the downside of the work I do is that there aren't many positions like mine available, and it can be hard to find a job. Also, it's hard on your family when you spend so much time in the field.

WHAT YOU SHOULD KNOW:

First, don't let yourself be pigeonholed by higher

education. I was told that I could either be a doctor or a lawyer — or go into business with my father. That was it. Most kids I knew who were interested in nature became doctors, but I didn't want to do that. Instead, by doing things in an unorthodox manner, I stumbled onto work that I love.

To be an ethnobotanist, you have to like people. Some of the local people are flattered when you ask them to share their wisdom, while others are more skeptical. Generally, though, if you show them that you mean no harm and want to learn, they're very happy to teach you what they know.

This work can be a lot of fun, but don't expect an easy ride. You have to be willing to be uncomfortable — to sleep in a hammock, drink muddy water, and eat disgusting foods.

And you have to make your own way. You can't just hang up a shingle that says "Ethnobotanist" and expect people to come to you. You have to go out and find the work that needs to be done, as well as the funding to do it.

The pay depends on the people you work for. Some ethnobotanists work in the pharmaceutical industry, and they make good money, perhaps as much as $100,000 a year. Working for a nonprofit organization or a university, you'll earn much less, starting at about $20,000 a year.

Mark takes hundreds of photos on each of his trips.

"You need practical experience before you can start giving advice."

JILL STOREY

MANAGEMENT CONSULTANT

San Francisco, California

WHAT I DO:

I do consulting work for companies that are having problems in the areas of marketing, financing, and strategic planning. My job is to come up with workable solutions to their problems. I also give advice to companies that are planning new ventures. For example, if a company has a new product, such as a new candy bar, I'll help them figure out the best way to market it, the customers they should target with their advertising, where the candy bar should be sold, and how much it should cost. Also, I work with them to determine how much money the company will need for the project and whether it's a worthwhile investment.

Much of my investigative work involves market research. This can include

Jill advises a client on how to develop a new product.

doing research in a library, phoning customers, or talking to other people in the business in order to scope out the competition. I try to learn everything that's going on in a particular industry so that I can advise my clients on the best approach for them to take.

I have a partner, and we work with about ten associates, each of whom is assigned to a specific project. At any given moment, I'm usually working with up to half a dozen clients. I might be drafting a business plan for one, working on financial projections for another, and meeting with a team of top managers for a third. And at the same time, I'll be writing proposals to bid on new work with other potential clients.

We specialize in working with socially responsible businesses, which are companies that have a product or service that can be con-

Jill does market research before advising clients.

sidered helpful to society. Often, it's an environmental product or service. For example, we've done work for one food company that uses rain forest ingredients and for another company that wholesales recycled paper.

HOW I GOT STARTED:

I went to business school and then took a job with a trucking company doing planning and financing. On the side, I did a little consulting, which had been an interest of mine while I was in business school. I gradually developed contacts until I had enough to go out on my own. A couple of years later, I took on a partner, and we moved into offices in the financial district here. Now we look like a real business.

HOW I FEEL ABOUT IT:

It's fun to work with lots of different businesses and so many different people. Each project is a new challenge for me. But even better than that, I get to work with a lot of people doing very interesting things with their businesses and their lives.

I feel very good about my work in many ways, but there are frustrations. Because there's so much variety, for example, I rarely get to delve too deeply into any one industry. Also, I don't get to implement my own recommendations. It can be frustrating when people choose not to do what I suggest, or they don't do it well.

WHAT YOU SHOULD KNOW:
An undergraduate degree in economics or some other business-related subject will probably give you a bit of an edge in this field, but it's not essential. My B.A., for instance, was in English.

Getting a graduate degree in business is a good idea, but again it's not essential unless you want to work for one of the top consulting firms. What is necessary is working in a business, almost any business, because you need practical experience before you can start giving advice.

On a personal level, you should have good conversational skills, because you're working directly with clients all the time. You must also be analytical, because you're always taking in information and processing it. And finally, if you plan to be self-employed, you should be willing to deal with change and uncertainty.

The money varies, depending on your experience and training. An entry-level researcher might make $30,000 a year, while a business school graduate at a mainstream management consulting firm might earn $70,000 a year. If you're working with a smaller firm, you should expect less, say about $40,000 a year.

Jill estimates how much a new venture will cost.

"I spend two or three years on each problem."

JOHN GARNETT
MATHEMATICIAN
Los Angeles, California

WHAT I DO:
As a math professor, I spend half my time teaching math classes — everything from introductory calculus to advanced graduate classes. The other half I spend researching mathematical problems. I like solving problems, and that's what I do for a living.

Most of my research involves complicated and theoretical problems, but there are some simpler ones that demonstrate what I do. For example, there's the Traveling Salesman Problem. In this problem, a traveling salesman has to visit twenty-five different villages, and he wants to minimize the time it takes to travel between them. In other words, the point is to find the shortest route. This problem deals with a finite space, because

John reviews a lesson plan for his advanced math class.

there are a limited number of villages. To solve it, you have to think of each village as a point in space. Things get tricky, however, when you expand the problem to include, say, ten million villages or an infinite number of villages. This is the kind of problem I do.

Some mathematicians prefer to devote themselves to one thing at a time, but I prefer to work on several problems at once. Also, some mathematicians work alone, while others collaborate with colleagues. In general, you find a great deal of collaboration in mathematics because conversation — whether at the coffee machine or at formal seminars — often suggests promising new approaches to problems.

Mathematicians themselves come in many different shapes and sizes. Some mathematicians are like artists in the way they excel

John looks on as two of his students play chess.

at creative thinking. Others are like lawyers, very verbal and logical.

HOW I GOT STARTED:
I've always liked logic and geometry problems. When I was a kid, I used to solve problems out of *Scientific American*. Mathematics was my favorite class in high school, and I couldn't wait to study math in college.

Once I got to college, however, I began to worry

that I wasn't talented enough to succeed in the field. But persistence helps, and hard work pays off.

HOW I FEEL ABOUT IT:
I love mathematics, but it can be very difficult work. I spend maybe two or three years on each problem. Once in a while I solve one, and I feel good about that. But a lot of days, I just fill up the waste basket with false leads. It's possible to spend an

entire year on a problem and not get anywhere with it. So mathematics isn't something you go into if you need instant gratification. It requires a great deal of patience.

Being a mathematician is a lot like being a writer. You sit there in front of an empty page and try to make something out of nothing. There's a lot of creativity in it, more than you might expect. Also, because the work is all in your head, it requires a great deal of discipline, just as writing does.

WHAT YOU SHOULD KNOW:

If you are really interested in this field, work at it while you're young — don't just wait until college. Like athletics, math requires skills and talents that can best be developed at an early age. It's also a subject in which you can become a real star while you're in your twenties. Some mathematicians become famous by the time they're twenty-five.

Also, training in mathematics can be very helpful even if you don't become a math professor. Math skills come into play in a wide variety of fields, from architecture to law to physics to economics.

In academia, the money is not outstanding, but you do have a certain amount of security. You may not make more than $50,000 or $60,000 a year, but you'll make it every year. If you're selling houses, you could make $500,000 one year, but only $20,000 the next.

John watches one of his students solve a problem.

"I can sell a $40,000 piece of glass over the phone."

ROBERTA DEAN
ANTIQUES DEALER

Laguna Beach, California

WHAT I DO:

I own and operate my own antiques store. I do most of the buying and selling, but my husband takes care of the bookkeeping, the inventory control, and our customer mailing list. I also give lectures, conduct estate sales, do appraisals, and participate in antiques shows throughout California.

My specialty is antique glass. Early on, even before I became an antiques dealer, I developed an interest in Early American pressed glass, which was the first commercial glass to be made in this country. In fact, glass was one of America's first industries, and now that original glass is very valuable. My knowledge of it attracts a lot of customers to the store. Once, for example, I went to an estate sale and bought a

glass sugar bowl for $4. When I got back to my shop, I authenticated the piece as an 18th-century, blown-mold, amethyst glass bowl in perfect condition. Later I sold it for considerably more than $4 to a lady in San Francisco, who is donating it to a museum.

Sometimes clients come to me with requests for particular pieces, which I locate and buy for them. That's the secret of being a successful dealer — having a regular group of clients who trust your judgment. I can call a client in Chicago, for instance, and sell him a $40,000 piece of glass over the phone because my clients know I'm looking out for them. They know that when I tell them a piece is in perfect condition, I mean it.

HOW I GOT STARTED:

I became interested in antiques around the age of

Roberta shows a client a silver serving dish.

12 when my aunt introduced me to Early American patterned glass. Soon I began studying antique glass by reading books on glass and visiting antiques stores to learn more about it. Then I got married and worked as a homemaker for many years, but I often thought about how much fun it would be to have my own antiques shop. Eventually I decided to open one. That was twenty-five years ago.

Everyone I knew said it was impossible just to open a store without working for someone else first, but I did it anyway. A lot of dealers are afraid to deal in glass because there are so many reproductions out there. Because that was my specialty, however, people began coming to me from all over the state to have their glass pieces appraised. My expertise in glass has helped me succeed because it truly is a specialty.

HOW I FEEL ABOUT IT:
I absolutely adore what I do. It's a love, not work at all. Nothing thrills me more than researching the origins of an old piece of glass or being called out to investigate the contents of an old, dust-covered trunk. And I love to

visit antiques shops and discuss antiques with other dealers.

Along the way, I've met some very interesting people. I sell to several major movie stars, including a famous comedian who collects presidential autographs. Once, I sold him a Thomas Jefferson letter, and he wrote me a beautiful note about how proud he was to own it.

I don't feel there are any real negatives to this work, but my husband gets tired of it sometimes. When we go on a trip, for instance, I insist on stopping at every antiques shop we pass.

WHAT YOU SHOULD KNOW: Get hold of books on antiques and start reading. The best books are the very specific ones. For example, if you want to learn about glass, get a book about a specific type of glass, such as Sandwich glass or Victorian glass. Also, go to museums. Try to visit a private collection so you can touch and hold the pieces. Feeling the glass in your hands helps you understand the difference between reproductions and the real thing. You should also try to find a friendly dealer. There are many wonderful people in this business who are interested in helping people learn more about antiques.

The money depends entirely on the quality of the antiques you sell. Some dealers make $30,000 at a weekend show. Others would be happy to make $200. Income also depends on your level of expertise. There's no limit to how much money you can make in this business, but you have to dedicate your life to it.

Roberta specializes in Early American glass.

"A lot of lawyers feel they're really writers at heart."

ROBERT YATES

MANAGING EDITOR

Chicago, Illinois

WHAT I DO:

As managing editor of the *American Bar Association Journal*, I run the magazine on a day-to-day basis. I used to be a practicing lawyer, but now I use my knowledge of the law to edit a journal for other lawyers. I make story assignments, check to be sure the other editors and reporters are working on their stories, and oversee the production of each issue.

Another part of my job involves developing story ideas. Because our readers are lawyers, we look for stories that are important to them, both as lawyers and as members of society. Our story ideas come from all over the place — from newspapers, from television shows, and from what's going on in the legal world.

One story I assigned recently details how the world of bankruptcy law has changed. Today many more bankruptcies are being filed than when I was practicing law. So I've assigned a writer to talk to some experts in order to find out why the situation has changed.

I've also just assigned a story on police brutality, because the issue has recently been in the news. It took us some time to find our own angle on the story — a take on it that would appeal to lawyers. But we finally came up with a story focusing on how police brutality relates to the criminal justice system as a whole.

In general, we try to analyze the ways in which widespread events and trends fit into the legal profession. We look for stories that have a news hook, with underlying legal issues that our readers would like explored. You can't

Robert develops story ideas for the magazine.

run a story in a vacuum. People read us for an analysis of what's happening.

HOW I GOT STARTED:

I had my own law practice for ten years, but then I got tired of it and instead decided to apply to journalism school. A lot of lawyers feel they're really writers at heart, and I was one of them. I had a feeling that I'd get more satisfaction from thinking and writing about the law than I would from plugging along every day, trying to help people solve their legal problems.

I spent a year getting a master's degree in journalism. Then I worked for a year and a half at a local newspaper covering the federal courts. Finally I got the managing editor's job here.

HOW I FEEL ABOUT IT:

I enjoy my work because it gives me the best of everything. I'm still involved with the law, which I find fascinating, but I don't have to put up with the grind of being a lawyer. Most lawyers don't get to try only the cases that interest them. When a client comes in with a problem, you have to deal with it. But as an editor, I do get to choose the issues I want to explore.

One thing I do miss about practicing law, however, is

the impact lawyers can have on peoples' lives. When you're in practice, you really are responsible for your clients. If you screw up in a criminal case, your client can go to prison. On the other hand, if you do your job well, you might really help someone. There's a direct effect lawyers have on people's lives that I don't have here.

WHAT YOU SHOULD KNOW:
If you're interested in writing as a career, then write. Submit something to a publication. You'll often get a critical response to your work, and that's how you learn. You can begin by writing for your school newspaper.

Many people who say they want to be writers think it has a dreamy quality. They think they can just sit down and write an article. But once they really try to write one, they see that it's hard work.

Money in this field has gotten a lot better than when I started. Journalism is an old-fashioned craft, with a "work your way up from the bottom" mentality. You typically have to start at a small-town paper, where the pay may be $14,000 a year to start. By the time you get to a magazine of our size, how-ever – we have a circulation of 400,000 – the pay im-proves a lot. In a mid-level editorial position, you'll make around $40,000 a year.

Robert checks with a reporter about an article.

"A lot of my ideas develop out of personal need."

LAURA FLAX

INVENTOR

Beverly Hills, California

WHAT I DO:

I invent new products, manufacture them, and bring them to market. I've developed all sorts of products, from toys to kitchen appliances to automotive accessories. People often say, "They should come up with something that does such and such." Well, I'm "they."

A lot of my ideas develop out of personal need. For example, you often see women commuting to work wearing sneakers because they're comfortable, but sneakers don't look good with a skirt. To solve this problem, I came up with a pair of women's shoes that have interchangeable heels, so you can easily turn your flats into pumps and back again. And I invented the Bug Sucker, a small vacuum shaped like an anteater. Now,

Laura makes a sketch for a new product she's designing.

I'm working on a pot that automatically stirs food while it's cooking.

Coming up with an idea, refining it, and developing a prototype is only about 20 percent of the work. The rest is getting the product into the marketplace. A lot of inventors are afraid to talk about what they're working on because someone might steal the idea. But I think you have to make people aware of your ideas. You have to be a marketer, even if it means taking a risk.

HOW I GOT STARTED:

I began as a math major in college, but I always enjoyed art and making things. At times, it seemed as though the world was saying I had to pick one or the other — either I had to be rational or creative. But I liked both fields, and I couldn't see why I should have to choose between them.

Laura develops a presentation for her new invention.

After college, I entered a graduate program in engineering at Stanford, looking for something "practical." But while I was there, I found there was a product design department, a joint program in mechanical engineering and art. I was very excited to find a program that combined my interests, so I transferred into it.

This program taught me a lot about the design process. I learned brainstorming techniques, how to interact with users, and I even got to work in a machine shop, building actual products. It was great hands-on experience, and it really motivated me. I also took business courses and went to trade shows to learn marketing and sales. Eventually I started my own company.

HOW I FEEL ABOUT IT: Inventing is very exciting work. It's never routine. I meet all sorts of different people, and I'm always working on different projects. But it's tremendously hard work. I usually have a dozen things going on all at once because I know that most of my ideas won't work out. If I come up with a thousand ideas, maybe a hundred of those will be worth pursuing, maybe ten will get fleshed out, and maybe one will actually make it into a store.

The biggest problems with this business are the high risk and the uncertainty. You can work on a project for years, and then somebody else comes out with it ahead of you. Once I was working on a product, and someone else came out with the same product with the same name! You have to be prepared for these kinds of setbacks so you can learn from them and keep going.

You also have to know when to stop working on something. For example, let's say you have a great idea, and people love it, but you find that there's no way to make money on it. If that's the case, you have to be able to walk away.

WHAT YOU SHOULD KNOW:
It's a good idea to bounce your ideas off other people, especially experts. There are associations of inventors, which are usually helpful, and there is an annual inventors convention in California. There are also trade shows, such as electronics or housewares shows, that you can visit to get ideas. And a lot of schools now offer design programs with an entrepreneurial focus.

Financially, there's plenty of risk in going into this business. That's why a lot of inventors work for computer firms and other engineering-related companies instead. Someone with a master's degree in design and engineering might earn $40,000 a year to start at one of those places.

PAUL RICHARD WARREN
PHILOSOPHER
Miami, Florida

WHAT I DO:

As an assistant professor of philosophy, my work involves teaching, research, and some administrative duties. I also write articles about my research and go to meetings and conventions of philosophers. My research concerns social and political philosophy, particularly as these subjects relate to the works of the philosopher Karl Marx.

Philosophers are people who think about abstract conceptual questions, such as "What is the nature of time?" Our studies are less defined than those of other academic disciplines. For example, historians study historical events. A historian might ask, "Why did Napoleon decide to invade Russia?" But a philosopher would ask "What is the meaning of history?"

Paul teaches an introductory class in political philosophy.

Analysis is part of what a philosopher does. People use words like *freedom* and *beauty* all the time. You hear them on television and read them in newspapers. But what do these words really mean? In my introductory class, I try to get students thinking about these sorts of conceptual issues.

HOW I GOT STARTED:

I've always been drawn to abstract questions. Even in high school, I was interested in philosophical thinking. And when I went to college, I took mostly philosophy and religion courses. After college, I found myself more interested in philosophy than in religious studies, so I decided to go to graduate school in philosophy and become a professor.

HOW I FEEL ABOUT IT:

I like my work a lot. Researching and writing

Paul discusses philosophy with a colleague.

philosophy promotes good mental discipline. And I also enjoy teaching because of the philosophical discussions I get to have with my students and with faculty colleagues.

The part I don't like is the grading. Reading essay after essay can be very tiring, and in grading them, it's sometimes hard to make fine distinctions. How do you decide, for example, between a B and a B-?

WHAT YOU SHOULD KNOW:
Philosophy is a good major, but I would recommend combining it with another, more practical major. Philosophy will give you many insights into that other subject, whether it be biology, history, or whatever. But you will also learn critical skills and how to analyze an argument,

which will improve your communication skills.

You don't need a degree to practice philosophy, however. Anybody can do it any time. When you sit with your friends and talk about the meaning of life, you're doing what a philosopher does. And when you read literature, philosophical questions inevitably come up. But you do need an advanced degree in philosophy to teach it.

As for money, an entry-level teaching position at this university pays $31,000 a year. There are regular increases, but nothing major unless you develop a prestigious reputation by writing such acclaimed books that many schools want to hire you. At that point, salaries become negotiable, but there are very few philosophers who ever get there.

Related Careers

Here are more research-related careers you may want to explore:

AEROSPACE ENGINEER
Aerospace engineers design, develop, and test airplanes, missiles, and spacecraft.

CRIMINOLOGIST
Criminologists investigate the social conditions that promote criminal behavior. They also study how effective punishments are in reducing criminal activity.

CRYPTOLOGIST
Cryptologists decipher secret messages and other texts written in code.

ECONOMIST
Economists study the way people do business to determine how society's resources can be most effectively managed.

FUTURIST
Futurists examine current social, political, and economic trends in order to make predictions about the future.

HISTORIAN
Historians research and analyze events in the past.

INVESTIGATIVE JOURNALIST
Investigative journalists research complex, and sometimes scandalous, news stories for newspapers as well as television and radio news programs.

LINGUIST
Linguists study both human speech and the structure and development of language.

MEDICAL RESEARCHER
Medical researchers conduct experiments to find new and better treatments for diseases.

PSYCHOLOGIST
Psychologists analyze human feelings and behavior to discover what motivates people to act in particular ways.

ROBOTICS ENGINEER
Robotics engineers design computer-controlled machines, or robots, that are used in factories to perform repetitive tasks.

SOCIOLOGIST
Sociologists study the interactions that occur among organized groups of people.

Organizations

Contact these organizations for information
about the following careers:

ANTHROPOLOGIST
American Anthropological Association
1703 New Hampshire Avenue, N.W., Washington, DC 20006

OPINION RESEARCHER
American Association for Public Opinion Research
P.O. Box 17, Princeton, NJ 08542

PHILOSOPHER
American Association of Philosophy Teachers
University of Oklahoma, P.O. Box 26901, Oklahoma City, OK 73190

URBAN ARCHAEOLOGIST
American Institute for Archaeological Research
24 Cross Road, Mt. Vernon, NH 03057

ETHNOMUSICOLOGIST
American Musicological Society
201 South 34th Street, Philadelphia, PA 19104

PHILOSOPHER
American Philosophical Society
104 South Fifth Street, Philadelphia, PA 19106

URBAN ARCHAEOLOGIST
Archaeological Institute of America
675 Commonwealth Avenue, Boston, MA 02215

SPECIAL WARFARE OFFICER
Association of Military Colleges and Schools of the U.S.
9115 McNair Avenue, Alexandria, VA 22309

ASTROPHYSICIST
Association of Universities for Research in Astronomy
1625 Massachusetts Avenue, N.W., Suite 701, Washington, DC 20036

MANAGEMENT CONSULTANT
Financial Analysts Federation
P.O. 3726, 5 Boar's Head Lane, Charlottesville, VA 22903

ANTIQUES DEALER
National Association of Dealers in Antiques
P.O. Box 421, Barrington, IL 60011

ASTROPHYSICIST
Universities Space Research Association
10227 Wincopin Circle, Suite 212, Columbia, MD 21044

Books

CAREER CHOICES FOR STUDENTS OF ECONOMICS
By Career Associates. New York: Walker & Co., 1985.

CAREER CHOICES FOR STUDENTS OF MATHEMATICS
By Career Associates. New York: Walker & Co., 1985.

CAREERS ENCYCLOPEDIA
Homewood, Ill.: Dow-Jones Irwin, 1980.

CAREERS IN SCIENCE
By Thomas A. Easton. Chicago: National Textbook Co., 1984.

THE COMPLETE GUIDE TO ENVIRONMENTAL CAREERS
By the CEIP Fund. Washington, D.C.: Island Press, 1989.

CREATIVE CAREERS
By Gary Blake and Robert W. Bly. New York: John Wiley, 1985.

THE ENCYCLOPEDIA OF CAREER CHOICES FOR THE 1990S
By Career Associates. New York: Walker & Co., 1991.

JOBS FOR THE 21ST CENTURY
By Robert V. Weinstein. New York: Collier Books, 1983.

OCCUPATIONAL OUTLOOK HANDBOOK
Washington, D.C.: U.S. Department of Labor, 1990.

OFF BEAT CAREERS
By Al Sacharov. Berkeley, Ca.: Ten Speed Press, 1988.

SPACE CAREERS
By C. Sheffield and C. Rosin. New York: William Morrow, 1983.

VGM'S CAREERS ENCYCLOPEDIA
Lincolnwood, Ill.: VGM Career Horizons, 1988.

Glossary Index

anthropologist, 30

antiques dealer, 46

appraisal — the estimation of the value of property by an authorized person, 47

artifact — an object, such as a tool or utensil, that indicates the technological development of the society from which it came, 7, 9, 31

astrophysicist, 18

conservatory — a school specializing in the study of the fine arts, particularly music, 12-13

detective, 26

entrepreneur — a person who organizes, manages, and assumes the risks of a business enterprise, 57

ethnobotanist, 34

ethnomusicologist, 10

fieldwork — work done in the field to gain practical experience through firsthand observation, 11, 31

inventor, 54

linguistics — the study of human speech, including the structure and nature of language, 13

management consultant, 38

managing editor, 50

mathematician, 42

meteor — a small particle in the solar system seen as a streak of light when it falls into the earth's atmosphere, 19

morgue — a place where dead bodies are kept until they are identified, 27

opinion researcher, 22

pawnshop — a place where people leave property as collateral for a loan, 27

philosopher, 58

planetarium — a building in which images of the solar system are projected on the ceiling to resemble the night sky, 21

refugee — one who flees a foreign country or power to escape danger or persecution, 11-12

sampling — selecting a group of people to serve as representatives of a larger group, 23

special warfare officer, 14

urban archaeologist, 6